NOT Just a Princess!

By Mary Lee

NOT Just a Princess!

By Mary Lee

"Good morning, Princess!" Mia's dad
called early one summer morning.

Normally, Mia loved playing princess,
but not today.

At breakfast, she was a lioness that only ate Jungle Crunchies. Her mom asked her wild guest to use a spoon.

When she arrived at the playground, Mia decided she was a pirate looking for a place to bury her treasure. She loved saying, "Arrr" and "There be treasure near, Matey."

After Mia dug a hole in the perfect spot, her mom decided it was time for a bath.

"This is one muddy princess we have here," she said.

Later, a mermaid and a starfish
invited Mia for tea under the sea.

She had to leave the party early,
before she turned into a sea-raisin.

During quiet time, she colored Cowgirl
Mia riding a unicorn, herding cattle
through the desert.

But Mia didn't want to be a princess,
a tigress, a pirate, a deep sea explorer
or a cowgirl.

She thought and thought...
what could she be?

Soon, she was so tired of thinking,
she fell asleep.

In her dreams, she was
racing rainbow-swans across
the mountaintops.

She was in the lead, almost to the finish line, when...

"Princess! Nap time's over. Time to go shopping," her mom called.

While Mia tried on a new dress, the saleslady remarked, "This is a dress for a princess!" Suddenly, Mia liked her old clothes better.

At the salon, her hair was made beautiful, her nails sparkling, but her smile went missing when someone said, "Awe, what a beautiful princess."

Mia's mom asked, "What's wrong, sweetie?"

"There's so many good things to be, and I just don't feel like a princess today!" Mia said sadly.

"You have a wonderful imagination, sweetie. No matter what you want to be, I will love you the same," her mom replied, holding her tight.

Mia felt better as she was tucked into bed later that night. "Goodnight, Nurse Mommy," Mia said smiling.

Mia's mom kissed her forehead and replied, "Goodnight, Doctor Mia."

As she drifted off to sleep, Mia thought she liked the sound of her new title, at least until the morning.

If you liked this book,
please take a moment to review.
Thank you!

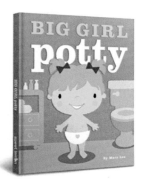

sweet lemon

Check out more Sweet Lemon Books at
sweetlemonbooks.com

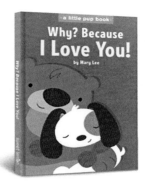

Check us out on social media.

Facebook
facebook.com/sweetlemonbooks

Twitter
twitter.com/sweetlemonbooks

Instagram
instagram.com/sweetlemonbooks

Pinterest
pinterest.com/sweetlemonbooks

46446628R00021

Made in the USA
Middletown, DE
01 August 2017